Contents

The Crossing	Page 3
The Land of the Long White Cloud	Page 29
Glossary	Page 56

SERVICE

0 6 JAN 2012

Written by Paul Mason
Illustrated by Carl Pearce

Published by Pearson Education Limited, Edinburgh Gate, Harlow, Essex, CM20 2JE
Registered company number: 872828

www.pearsonschools.co.uk

Text © Paul Mason 2011

Designed by Bigtop
Original illustrations © Pearson Education 2011
Illustrated by Carl Pearce

The right of Paul Mason to be identified as author of this work has been asserted by him in
accordance with the Copyright, Designs and Patents Act 1988.

First published 2011

15 14 13 12 11
10 9 8 7 6 5 4 3 2 1

British Library Cataloguing in Publication Data
A catalogue record for this book is available from the British Library

ISBN 978 1 408 27391 3

Copyright notice
All rights reserved. No part of this publication may be reproduced in any form or by any means
(including photocopying or storing it in any medium by electronic means and whether or not
transiently or incidentally to some other use of this publication) without the written permission
of the copyright owner, except in accordance with the provisions of the Copyright, Designs and
Patents Act 1988 or under the terms of a licence issued by the Copyright Licensing Agency, Saffron
House, 6¬10 Kirby Street, London EC1N 8TS (www.cla.co.uk). Applications for the copyright
owner's written permission should be addressed to the publisher.

Printed and bound at Ashford Colour Press

Acknowledgements
We would like to thank the children and teachers of Bangor Central Integrated Primary School,
NI; Bishop Henderson C of E Primary School, Somerset; Brookside Community Primary School,
Somerset; Cheddington Combined School, Buckinghamshire; Cofton Primary School, Birmingham;
Dair House Independent School, Buckinghamshire; Deal Parochial School, Kent; Newbold
Riverside Primary School, Rugby and Windmill Primary School, Oxford for their invaluable help in
the development and trialling of the Bug Club resources.

Every effort has been made to contact copyright holders of material reproduced in this book. Any
omissions will be rectified in subsequent printings if notice is given to the publishers.

Watching the Clouds

The decision to leave your home is a hard one to make. You are giving up what you know for a future that is uncertain. Yet when I was only a young girl, my **whānau** made that difficult choice. We chose to cross the oceans to join the others of our people who had gone in search of a new home and a better life. This is how I remember that brave crossing …

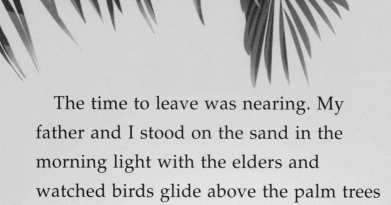

The time to leave was nearing. My father and I stood on the sand in the morning light with the elders and watched birds glide above the palm trees and out over the waves. **Matua** and I stared until they were nothing more than tiny points in the sky. Soon we would follow. The **waka** was ready, its sails eager for wind.

Though the journey was full of danger, many of our people had already left this island for a new land. In the breeze, I shivered. My grandfather began to sing in a low, clear voice, his eyes bright. **Koro** sang of roaming birds, soaring above the sea, chasing a path over drifting waves. It was an old song.

Taine, the wisest of our village, kept his gaze on the sky. He waited till Koro stopped singing, then spoke. "The clouds in the distance are gathering," he said, his voice a whisper.

Matua followed his eyes. "It is true." He shook his head. "Must we hold the boat?" He was disappointed.

"**Āe**," Taine muttered. "But maybe soon the ocean will receive you more kindly." He shuffled off with the others back to the village. "You must check again that everything is ready."

Koro put his arm on Matua's shoulder. "What is another day or two, my son?" he said. "Remember, after the storm comes a rainbow."

Matua grumbled. I knew he itched to be at sea. Instead, he and Koro discussed the path we would take, even though they both knew it as they knew their own palms.

My **māmā** was Lani, named after
the sky, and just as beautiful. She and
the others gathered food. There were
coconuts, **kūmara** and **taro**. Two whole
pigs had been baked, fish had been dried.
Gourds full of water were already on the
boat. We could be at sea for many days
on this long crossing. We would carry
animals and plants to help us begin life
in the new land.

In truth, we had collected as much as could be spared. The island herself did not have much to give. As our people had grown, food had become scarce. It was for this that we journeyed across the wide sea. I thought about how I would miss our home.

I sat with the **wāhine** and helped them as they wove and talked in the sunshine. How I loved their stories! I fed the chickens and the pigs that would come with us on the boat. I swam with my friends, the ones who would not be coming.

I wanted to be with them for as long as I could. We shrieked as we splashed in the water and chased each other on the shore. But inside I knew we were all carrying broken hearts. I gave them necklaces I had made from shells and sharks' teeth so that they might remember me.

On the beach I overheard some of the boys tell each other in hushed voices about those of our people who had gone to sea not to return. My thoughts were troubled for the rest of that day.

Leaving Home

On the evening of our departure, I observed Taine and Koro as they stared at the sunset, taking note of its path. They marked out the horizon – watching the stars that winked in the darkening sky. They had set the passage we would take. Everything had been placed in the waka. Feathers flapped on the masts, telling us the wind was true.

Koro talked with Taine and I saw Taine nod. He had given his approval. Koro clapped his hands, eyes dancing. "It is a good time to sail!" he shouted to us. It was the decision we had been waiting for! We cheered and hugged each other.

Our village was soon gathered on the sand to wish us good fortune on our voyage. Three families were travelling on the boat – almost twenty souls would ride the waves to a distant land. There were many tears, from fear and sadness.

The waka rocked on the waves, the oars at the **helm** ready to steer us, the two **prows** curved and proud. We waded through the warm water and climbed on board. I helped my little brothers.

From the shore came a mournful song. A song of parting. We would not see each other again. Even much later, over the fluttering of the sails, I could still hear voices carried on the breeze.

To begin with, all was well.

The wind and current were kind and we flew across the water, the **hulls** of the canoe cutting through the waves like two dolphins. We passed nearby islands and were soon out of sight of any land, and so it was for days. Nothing but the rolling blue of the sea.

Koro was our navigator. His feet were planted firmly on the deck, feeling any changes in the sea. He kept his eyes to the distance, watching the shape of the waves, reading the current of the water. He determined the direction of the wind

from the way the feathers blew on the
mast. When dusk came, he waited for the
stars to reveal the way, and all the time
shouting instructions.

Matua and another took the steering
oars, one on each hull. Others manoeuvred
the sails, letting them out or making them
strong. There was always excited chatter,
and we were in good heart.

On the platform that strode the two
hulls was a hut where we could shelter
if the sky became angry. Just outside, a
cooking fire burned cheerfully in a trough

of sand. It was my task to make sure it never went out. I would lean on Māmā's warm shoulder, breaking twigs to feed to the hungry embers, speaking to the flames as I worked.

Even though our boat was solid, the sea found ways to creep in. Water had to be bailed night and day. I took my turn sitting down in the hole, scooping out water. Then there were the animals to feed and the plants we carried with us had to be watered. The sails needed to be mended. We all shared the chores. My friends and I sat and chatted about what our new homeland would be like.

"Kura, sitting is not working," Māmā would tease me.

"I work hard, Māmā," I would protest, and then she would give me one of her smiles.

"Āe, I know. Now go and tell your father he must come and eat."

The Storm

It was many nights into our voyage and good fortune was still with us. The wind was warm, and the sky clear. The roll of the swell was gentle beneath the boat. I watched how the light from the moon played along the water.

But one night, as I stood with Koro, the sea went dark. Cruel waves broke against the boat. The feathers hanging from the mast rattled in the wind. "Is there a storm coming?" I asked.

"Āe, **Tāwhiri-mātea** becomes annoyed," Koro grumbled. "Be strong on the oar!" he called to the man at the helm. "Drop the light anchor to steady the boat."

It was going to get rough.

For an age, we battled against the storm. Lightning jagged across the dark sky, followed by a boom of thunder that ripped through the boat. We climbed over giant wave after giant wave, tumbling down the other side. We pitched and rolled. Four men were on the oars at the back; another two at the front. Koro bellowed instructions until his voice was raw. Watching from the hut, I wanted to help him. I pushed outside and tried to leap from the deck to the hull where Koro stood.

I did not make it.

My legs cracked into the wood and I dropped, arms grabbing hopelessly. I yelled out. With a smack I hit the sea.

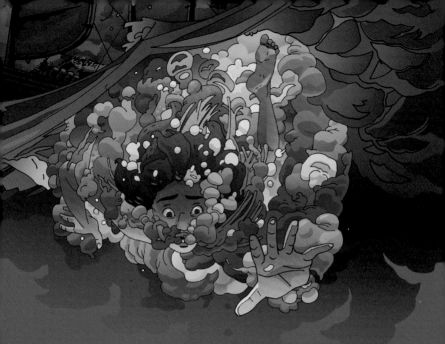

Hurled like a stone into the dark water.

I slammed against the side of the waka. There was a roar as I went under. Water stung my eyes and grabbed at my throat. My hands clawed this way and that. Over and over I rolled. Everything began to go dark.

Then I felt a hand take hold of me. Someone in the water gripped my hair and pulled me above water. Powerful arms wrapped around me. I gasped for breath. That much I recall.

When I woke, I was in the hut, Māmā leaning over me.

"Ah, she wakes!" she smiled, but her eyes were red with tears. "We almost lost you to the sea."

My head hurt. I felt a large lump under my hair. My legs ached. "What happened?"

"You tried to jump and missed. You were thoughtless, but that doesn't matter

now. Here, drink this," and she gave me some coconut milk.

Matua was there too. His face was like stone.

"Be glad you have a strong head of hair, or I may never have saved you," he growled.

"I'm sorry, Matua", I said, and he managed a smile.

When I felt strong enough, I went on deck to join the others. Some were bailing water out of the boat. One person was up the mast, keeping watch on the water. The sea was still angry.

Koro felt every wave that hit our boat through his exhausted legs; he watched the wind for any sign of change. He was at one with the sea and the sky; it was the way of our people. In that storm, he called on everything he had ever learned to steer us through.

At last, on the evening of the second day, the sea settled. The wind dropped down, the waves no longer pitched themselves against the canoe. All was calm. We were weak, but still we were able to grin.

Only Koro and Matua did not smile. They looked at the sky, still wrapped in a blanket of grey.

"I fear the storm has taken us off our course," Matua shook his head. "And again we will not see the stars to guide us tonight."

Koro patted Matua on the arm. "We will discover the way. Something tells me."

Guides from the Deep

That night, it happened as Koro said it would. Though cloud still concealed the stars from us, the moonlight was bright. From one of the men standing watch on the **bow** came a joyful shout that brought us to our feet.

"**Paikea**!" He called, "Paikea!"

Whales. Our brothers and sisters of the deep.

The whales broke the surface not three boat-lengths away from us, their bodies glistening and dark, water bursting from their blowholes. In front of us they glided, a group like our own, migrating across the ocean to cooler waters. We hailed them as they swam away towards the horizon. Such an omen!

The men on the oars did not have to be told. Together they directed the boat to follow the whales, travelling in their wake. Our friends played with us now, leaping out of the ocean and plunging back down, sending sprays of water high into the night sky. They lifted their tails as if to say, "This way little brothers. We will show you."

Koro grinned. "All we need do now is shadow them on their journey. They will lead us near land."

Some days later, when the sun was halfway through its passage, we saw birds. Birds that fly out to sea at day and return to land at night. We knew then that we would make landfall.

Our crossing was almost at an end. Māmā clasped me close to her. We would arrive before evening. With good fortune, we would find the village of those that had gone before us. What would our new home be like?

As I stared out at the ocean, searching for land, I thought about our voyage. How the gale had sent waves to pound the boat. How the sea had almost claimed my life. I could see Matua and Koro, sturdy and skilful, as they guided us across the ocean. I remembered, too, the island we had left behind.

Then we saw clouds in the distance. The type of clouds that tells us land lies underneath. We were close!

"A prize to the first person who catches sight of land!" shouted Koro, grinning.

I still wear the prize, this necklace, even now, to remind me of how we reached this abundant land. Though the journey was difficult and could have ended in disaster, we survived, as do our people to this day ...

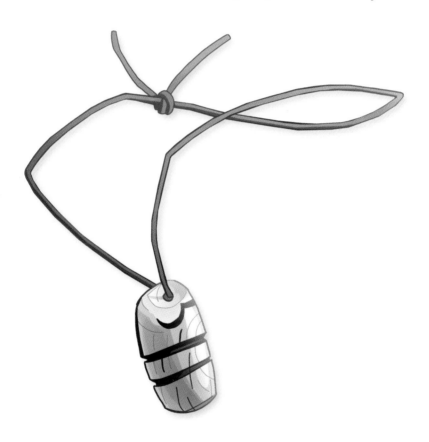

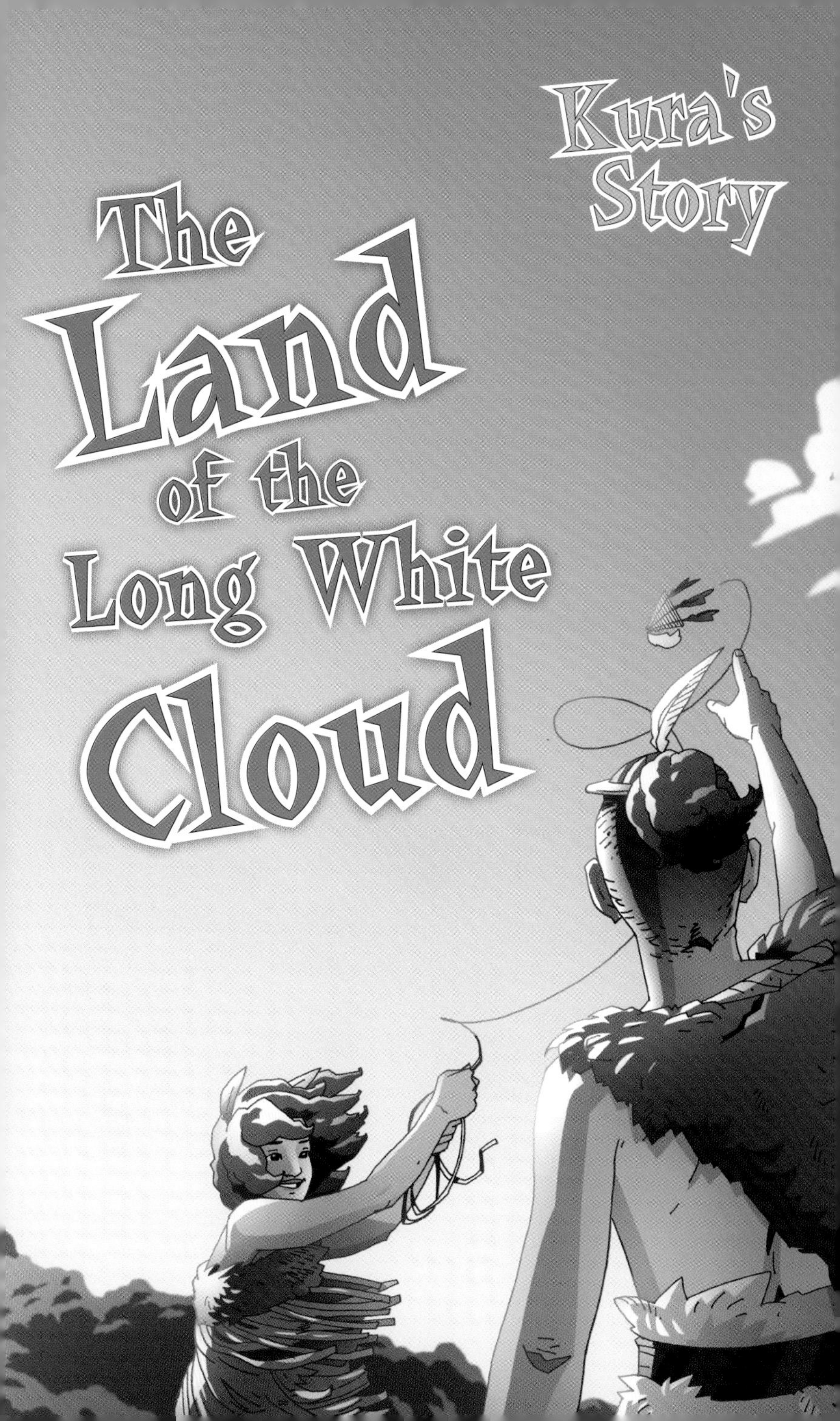
Kura's Story
The Land of the Long White Cloud

The Beach

You must learn this, child: when I was only a little girl myself, our **whānau** sailed over the sea to join the others in this place. What a voyage that was! I will never forget how it felt to finally reach this beautiful land.

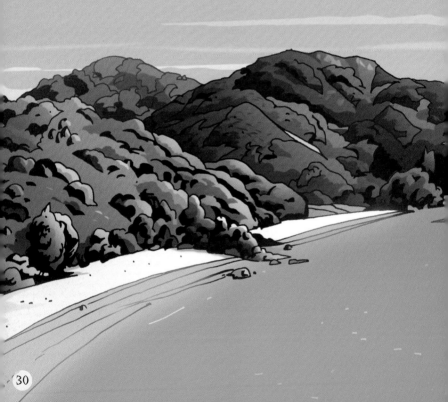

Arriving here was like a blessing. There were forests full of birds for the pot, our harvests were rich, and my friend Tama and I often gathered food from the sea ...

We were in the clear water, pulling mussels off the rocks when the stingray came. It was Tama who saw it first, gliding straight towards our legs, wings rolling.

"Get out!" he said quickly. "I don't want to feel the bite of its tail."

We scrambled onto the rocks, and I felt a stinging sensation. In my hurry I had cut my knee, but I was fascinated by the creature. "Run and get your spear and you can catch it."

"For a girl, Kura, you certainly have a hunter's spirit!" Tama smiled and shook his head. "There is no need to catch the stingray. Better to leave it to go about its day."

The brown shape rippled over the sand. Tama was right – it was beautiful. The creature's wings flapped gently, its tail sliding behind as it looked for food along the ocean bottom. We watched until the stingray slipped through a hole in the rock and was gone.

"Come, let us go back to the village," I said, lifting the bag of mussels. "We still have to clean these."

Our village was not far from the shore, just a short walk inland, close to the forest. A thin fence made of sticks ran around our homes and **kumara** fields.

The kitchens were away from the other shelters, and Tama and I took our catch there. **Māmā** and some of the others were preparing the evening meal.

"Kura, look at your knee! How did you get this one?" Māmā shook her head.

"On the rocks. We saw a stingray and jumped."

"Come here." Māmā smiled as she cleaned my leg. "Well, I hope you got lots of mussels. I would hate for this cut to have been for nothing."

"The bag is almost full."

"Good work," said Māmā as she examined our catch. "We'll eat well."

Tama and I got to work. If we were quick, we would still have time to fly our kite before nightfall.

The tide was out by the time we made it back to the beach. Waves broke in the distance. In the fading sun, the sand stretched before us, shiny and firm – our playground.

"Watch out, Kura! The kite is dropping!" Tama shouted.

I gave the line a strong tug and pulled it in, hand over hand. Our kite cut through the air like a spear, the frame whistling through the sky.

Some of the others joined us. Soon there were three or four kites in the air. My father came to stand with us. After a hard day fishing, **Matua**'s eyes eagerly followed the kite.

"Here," I said. "Take a turn."

Matua smiled and took the line from me, then turned towards Tama. "Some of us are leaving to hunt moa tomorrow, Tama. We would like you to come."

A grin spread across Tama's face. "Really?"

"I have seen you practising with your spear. Your father and I think you are ready."

"I am ready!" Tama laughed.

"Good. Then it is settled."

Tama ran off down the beach whooping and cheering, to tell the other boys; to boast that he was going to bring home a moa. My cheeks burned. It wasn't fair.

"I could also use a spear if you would let me." I looked up at Matua, but I knew as the words left my mouth that it was hopeless.

Matua laughed and ruffled my hair.

"You're a brave one, my girl, but you should stick to kite-flying. Besides, you will have work to do too," he said.

Tama came running back down to us, but when he noticed how disappointed I was, he stopped smiling. He punched me playfully on the arm. Now I felt ashamed. In truth, I was happy for him.

"Just watch out that a moa doesn't trample on you with its big feet!" I said to him, managing a smile.

Left Behind

On the day the men went to hunt, Ahu, one of the **kuia**, took me to harvest **harakeke** so that we could weave. I dragged my feet as I followed behind her down the path. By now Tama would probably be hiding in the long grass, spear in his hand, waiting for the giant birds to pass near. When they came close enough, he would leap out and hurl his spear … If only I could be there too.

"Kura! Pay attention. You are not with me," Ahu broke me from my daydream. "Child, you must learn the old ways, so that you too can one day pass them on." She smiled at me. "You know, hunting is not the only important thing in the world."

Embarrassed, I nodded. Now, I watched her as she worked. Ahu first gave a prayer of thanks before she cut into the plant. She handled the leaves gently as she talked, her wrinkled face old and soft – though the tattoo below her chin had not faded with time.

"Remember, you must cut the leaves downward, always downward so that they will grow again."

I nodded. "Yes, kuia."

"And what else do you know?"

"Never cut the heart out of the plant. Never cut more than you need."

"**Āe**, good girl. Now come, there's work to be done."

I sat with Māmā and the others, and we wove. It was good to be in the sunshine, to hear their laughter. Ahu was weaving skilfully. Her fingers were old, but they danced quickly.

She reached for her pouch and carefully took out a handful of feathers. She attached some along the edge of a cloak.

"We must use these carefully, these feathers."

"Why?" I asked.

"They are moa feathers. Not so many moa these days. Once there were plenty." The others made sounds of agreement.

"Why are there so few, kuia?"

"Perhaps it is because we have not treated the moa like we treat the harakeke." She muttered, "Maybe we have taken too much."

Ahu was right. A few days later, the men returned from their hunting trip with only a few smaller birds and no moa. Their spirits were as empty as their baskets.

"We couldn't find any," Tama said, his mouth thin. "My spear did not get used."

"I'm sorry that we came back with little to show, son." His father shook his head. "We were unlucky, but there will be other times, you'll see."

I took Tama by the hand. "Come. Never mind about hunting. The wind is good for kite-flying."

But that did not go well either. A strong gust came and pulled at our kite, more than the line could bear. With a snap, the kite broke free and soared off towards the forest. We gave chase for a time, but it flew on until we lost sight of it over the trees.

"You held the line too tight," Tama grumbled at me. "What a day this is turning out to be!"

"It wasn't my fault," I answered back, "and I don't see why you're so angry. At least you got a chance to hunt."

"Some chance," Tama muttered. He turned and headed back to the village.

I stood and looked towards the thick trees. Somewhere in there lay our kite, a gift for **Tāne-mahuta**.

The Forest

On the day that followed, I wanted to see if I could find our kite. I found Tama fishing and asked him if he wanted to come, but he was bad-tempered still and said he was too busy for such things. I told him that I didn't need his help. Seeing him sulking about nothing had made me annoyed again.

I followed the path that led into the forest. It was heavy with **ponga** and palm trees, and the green cloak above me blocked the sunlight. I looked about uneasily. I rarely ventured in here on my own.

I knew it was almost hopeless to find the kite here, but still I carried on up the hill. I would show Tama. A bird joined me – a **pīwakawaka**, hopping and fluttering on the path behind, watching to see if my footsteps brought out insects. Our people knew of such birds as bringers of bad news. I hoped it would stop following me.

I reached the top of the path and looked down to the plain below, where the forest ended. That was where the hunters had gone to find the moa, so I decided to follow their track for a while.

The path dropped steeply down towards the plain now, the ground loose in places. I lost my footing and slipped. I couldn't stop as the earth underneath me gave way. I tumbled down the hillside, twigs clawing at my skin. At last, with a thud, I stopped. I lay on the plain, where the long grass met the trees. I wept silently, wishing I had never come looking for that kite. Slowly, my aches began to subside, and I lay there for a time looking up at the sky.

It was then that I heard a noise. My arms and legs became stone, and my heart thumped. A low grunt; a tearing of grass. Too close for my liking. I rolled quietly onto my stomach, hardly daring to move.

I gasped. There in front of me, so close that I could see their bright eyes, were birds like giants. Some of them were taller and heavier than two men put together.

It was a group of moa, not more than a small canoe length away. My throat felt tight. They had no wings, but their legs were truly huge. The tops of their legs were like tree trunks, the toes on their feet strong, the claws sharp. I'd heard of someone from our tribe being trampled and kicked by these birds. They had broken his bones. Now I could believe it.

What would they do if they sensed me? Would they bolt? Would they kick me?

I stayed perfectly still and watched them as they passed by, grazing. What beasts! More splendid than anything I had seen before. I must stay hidden. I didn't want to startle them, to make them run.

Like a lizard, I crept behind some nearby harakeke. From my safe hiding place, I watched. My heart raced to see these enormous birds so close.

And there, on the grass beside them, as plain as day, was the kite! The kite that had escaped and led me here. Brought me to these moa!

The moa were bent over, heads low, ripping out and eating plants. They called to each other with low, deep sounds. Some stretched their necks up to the trees, looking for food, their beaks broad and hard. They snapped off thick twigs like they were straw.

It was then that I realised something. I should go and call the others; race back to the village and tell the hunters. They could come here with their dogs in time to catch these birds.

I pictured Tama and Matua telling me how clever and brave I was; how I had brought them a good hunt. Then the **hangi** in the village would be full. Yes, then they would all smile.

Nothing but Trees

I made to turn back and take the path up through the forest, but I paused to look at the birds one last time. Still they were grazing, the breeze rustling the grass and their soft, brown feathers. There were young moa too, perhaps only a year old, not full of feather yet, not straying far from the older ones. They looked so peaceful.

Watching them, I thought of something. Something Ahu had told me as we wove: "Not so many moa these days ..." she had said. "Once there were plenty."

Even though the sun shone on my back, hearing the words in my head made me feel cold. I looked at the gentle birds. Ahu's voice came again. "Maybe we have taken too much." I remembered too how I had wanted Tama to spear that stingray, but that he had said "No," and instead we had watched it glide beautifully through the water.

I made up my mind and turned to leave once again – to go back to the village.

I slipped away quietly without disturbing the moa. They didn't even know I had been there.

I reached the village before the sun had finished its journey across the sky. Light still played on the sea. Some of the others raced each other on the beach. I ran up to Tama.

"You're back," he grinned. I noticed he was no longer wearing a long face.

"How was the fishing?" I asked.

"I caught one this big in the shallows with my spear." Tama spread out his arms. "Sorry I was grumpy before."

"I'm sorry too."

Tama looked down at my empty hands and my scratched arms. "You didn't find the kite then?"

I shook my head. "There was nothing." I thought about the giant birds, the light in their eyes; the wind ruffling their feathers; grazing calmly in the grass without fear.

"No. Nothing but trees," I said with a smile.

Glossary

Āe: yes

Bow: front part of a boat

Hangi: traditional Māori earth oven

Harakeke: fibrous plant with long, thin leaves, important to Māori as a material for weaving and other things

Helm: steering part of a boat: the rudder or tiller

Hull: main part of a ship, including the bottom, sides and deck

Koro: term used to address an older man; grandfather

Kuia: elder woman

Kūmara: sweet potato, introduced to New Zealand from Polynesia

Māmā: mother

Matua: father

Paikea: humpback whale

Pīwakawaka: bird also known as a 'fantail' because of its tail that spreads out like a fan

Ponga: silver tree fern

Prow: front or forward part of the boat

Tāne-mahuta: god of the forest

Taro: starchy root vegetable used throughout the Pacific

Tāwhiri-mātea: god of wind and storms

Wāhine: women

Waka: canoe

Whānau: family